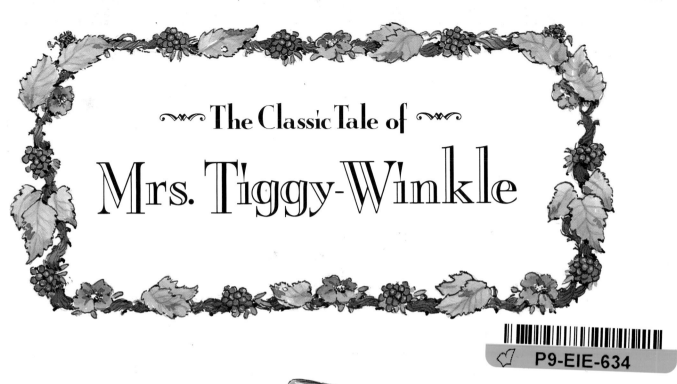

~ The Classic Tale of ~
Mrs. Tiggy-Winkle

Manufactured in U.S.A.

8 7 6 5 4 3 2 1

ISBN 1-56173-477-2

Cover illustration by Anita Nelson

Book illustrations by Sam Thiewes

Other illustrations by Pat Schoonover

Once upon a time there was a little girl named Lucie who lived on a farm. She was a good little girl, but she was always losing her pocket handkerchiefs!

One day little Lucie came into the farmyard crying, "I've lost my handkerchief! Three handkerchiefs and a pinafore! Have *you* seen them, Tabby Kitten?"

The kitten went on washing her white paws. Lucie asked a speckled hen, "Sally Henny-Penny, have *you* found three handkerchiefs?"

But the speckled hen ran into the barn clucking, "I go barefoot, barefoot, barefoot!"

Lucie climbed the steps in the garden wall and looked up at the hillside. She thought she saw some white things spread upon the grass.

Lucie scrambled up the hill as fast as her legs would carry her. She ran along a steep pathway—up and up. Soon she came to a spring bubbling out from the hillside. And where the sand upon the path was wet, there were footprints of a *very* small person.

The path ended under a big rock. The grass was short and green here. There were clotheslines of braided grasses hanging from stems and sticks; a heap of tiny clothespins was on the ground. But there were no handkerchiefs!

There was something else, though—a door! It led straight into the hill, and beyond it someone was singing:

"Lily-white and clean, oh!
With little frills between, oh!
Smooth and hot—red rusty spot
Never here be seen, oh!"

Lucie's knock interrupted the song. A frightened little voice called out, "Who's there?"

Lucie opened the door and gazed upon a nice clean kitchen. It was just like any other farm kitchen, except that the ceiling was so low that Lucie's head nearly touched it. The pots and pans were small, and so was everything else.

There, at the table with an iron in her hand, stood a very short, plump person staring anxiously at Lucie. Her print gown was tucked up, and she was wearing a large apron over her striped petticoat. Her little black nose went *sniffle, snuffle,* and her eyes went *twinkle, twinkle.* And underneath her cap—where Lucie had yellow curls—the little person had PRICKLES!

"Who are you?" asked Lucie. "Have you seen my pocket handkerchiefs?"

The little person curtsied. "Oh, yes, miss. My name is Mrs. Tiggy-Winkle." And she took something out of a clothes basket, and spread it on the ironing blanket.

"That's not my handkerchief," said Lucie.

"Oh, no, if you please, miss, that's a little red vest belonging to Cock Robin!" And she ironed it and folded it. Mrs. Tiggy-Winkle took another hot iron from the fire.

"There's one of my handkerchiefs!" cried Lucie. "And there's my pinafore!"

Mrs. Tiggy-Winkle ironed the pinafore and shook out the ruffles.

"Oh, that *is* lovely!" said Lucie.

"Are those yellow gloves?" asked Lucie.

"Oh, no! That's a pair of stockings belonging to Sally Henny-Penny. Look how she's worn out the heels from scratching in the barnyard! She'll very soon go barefoot!"

"And whose red handkerchief is this?"

"If you please, miss, it belongs to old Mrs. Rabbit. It *did* smell so of onions. I had to wash it separately," said Mrs. Tiggy-Winkle.

"What are these funny little white things?" asked Lucie.

"That's a pair of mittens belonging to Tabby Kitten. I only have to iron them, she washes them herself."

"Here are my other handkerchiefs!" said Lucie. And at last the basket was empty.

After they had sorted the wash, Mrs. Tiggy-Winkle made tea—a cup for herself and a cup for Lucie. She and Lucie sat on a bench in front of the fire and looked at one another.

Mrs. Tiggy-Winkle's hands were very, very brown, and very, very wrinkly from the soapsuds. And all through her gown and cap there were *hairpins* sticking wrong end out.

When they had finished tea, they tied up the clothes in bundles. Lucie's handkerchiefs were folded up inside her clean pinafore and fastened with a silver safety pin.

Then away down the hill trotted Lucie and Mrs. Tiggy-Winkle with the bundles of clothes. All the way down the path little animals came out of the woods to meet them. The very first they met were Peter Rabbit and Benjamin Bunny!

Mrs. Tiggy-Winkle and Lucie gave them all their nice clean clothes. The little animals and birds were very grateful to dear Mrs. Tiggy-Winkle.

At the bottom of the hill they came to the garden steps. There was nothing left to carry except Lucie's one little bundle.

Lucie scrambled up the steps with the bundle in her arms. Then she turned to say "Good night," and to thank the washerwoman.

But how *very* odd! Mrs. Tiggy-Winkle had not waited for thanks.

She was running, running, running up the hill—and where was her white ruffled cap? And her shawl? And her gown? And her petticoat?

And how small she seemed—and how brown—and covered with PRICKLES!

Why, Mrs. Tiggy-Winkle was nothing but a HEDGEHOG!

Now some people say that little Lucie had been sleeping and dreaming on the garden steps. But then how could she have found three clean handkerchiefs and a pinafore, all pinned with a silver safety pin?

And besides—*I* have seen that door in the hill called Cat Bells. And besides—*I* am a good friend of dear Mrs. Tiggy-Winkle!